PONY♥DAYS

SHELTIE
and the
Stray

Read all about Sheltie in these other Pony Days Books!

PONY❤DAYS

SHELTIE
and the
Stray

by Peter Clover

Cover illustration by
Tristan Elwell

AN
APPLE
PAPERBACK

SCHOLASTIC INC.
New York   Toronto   London   Auckland   Sydney
Mexico City   New Delhi   Hong Kong   Buenos Aires

ISBN 0-439-68890-6

12 11 10 9 8 7 6 5 4 3 2 1   5 6 7 8 9 10/0

Printed in the U.S.A.   40

First Scholastic printing, March 2005

Chapter One

It was a cold, frosty morning in Little
Applewood. Emma was out riding through
Bramble Wood on Sheltie, her little
Shetland pony.

Emma was on a mission. She was riding
Sheltie through the woods behind
Horseshoe Pond looking for wildlife.
Emma had chosen "Wildlife and
Woodlands" as her special school project

and was out riding extra early to see if she could spot anything unusual.

Sheltie was really excited about being out on a ride so early in the morning. His hot breath made little puffs of steam when he blew through his nostrils. And his shaggy mane bounced against his neck as he trampled through a thick carpet of autumn leaves.

Emma was wrapped up like a Christmas present in her warm, padded coat. She pulled back her glove and checked her watch. It was eight o'clock.

"Time to be heading back," said Emma. "Nothing much to report today, Sheltie. Not even a squirrel!"

Sheltie rustled his nose into a pile of leaves and gave a loud sneeze.

"Bless you!" said Emma. Then she

laughed as Sheltie uncovered a cluster of acorns.

"Thank you, Sheltie," she said. "But I've already got lots of acorns."

Sheltie tossed his head and snorted loudly. Then he began pawing at the ground with his hoof. Sheltie scraped away the covering of dry leaves and this time he pulled out a large chestnut.

"That's a whopper, Sheltie." Emma laughed. "I've got chestnuts, too, but none as big as that! It's the size of a tennis ball!"

Emma gave Sheltie a hearty pat on his neck and Sheltie swished his tail. This time the little pony seemed to know that he had found something special. Emma carefully picked up the giant chestnut and slipped it into her pocket.

As they trotted back through the woods, Emma kept a lookout for foxes, rabbits, hedgehogs, mice, and even badgers. Emma was *really* hoping that she might be lucky enough to see a badger, even though she knew that they mostly come out at night. She had Dad's camera tucked away in her big zippered pocket.

Then, just before they reached the edge of the woods, Sheltie stopped suddenly and flicked up his ears.

"What is it, boy?" asked Emma. Then she heard a twig snap behind her and turned around in the saddle.

Sheltie blew a snort and turned his head, too. They both looked, but there was nothing to see. Then Emma heard a rustling sound coming from behind a tree to their left. Sheltie's ears pricked up again and he blew softly.

"Shh, Sheltie!" whispered Emma. "There's something over there! It could be a fox." She unzipped her pocket and reached for the camera, then urged Sheltie to walk forward, very slowly.

Sheltie was staring at the spot where the noise was coming from. Emma held the camera ready.

Suddenly, there was a loud *bang* from the other side of the woods behind them. It was the sound of a shotgun firing and it made Emma and Sheltie jump.

Emma swung around again to look back in the direction of the shot. Whatever was rustling behind the tree dived for cover into the undergrowth.

"It must have been a rabbit," said Emma. "But whatever it was, it's gone now, Sheltie! Someone's out there shooting and scared it off."

As Emma tucked the camera back into her pocket, Sheltie jangled his bit impatiently.

"Come on, then, boy. Home!"

Sheltie walked on, and moments later they stepped out of the woods into the bright morning sunshine.

They saw a man walking some distance away with a shotgun cocked across his arm. The man was calling out to someone and kicking at the bushes with his boot as though he was looking for something. Emma didn't like the look of him at all.

"Let's stay here for a moment, Sheltie," she said, "and wait for that nasty man to

go." Emma didn't want to ride past him.
She thought he looked very unfriendly.
Emma didn't like men with shotguns.

Sheltie shook his head and jangled his
reins. Then he stood perfectly still and
waited for Emma to give him the
command to "walk on."

* * *

"He was horrible," Emma told Dad as she helped herself to toast at breakfast. "A big scruffy man shooting poor little rabbits. I should have taken his photograph and given it to the police."

"It's best not to think about it," said Mom. "People often get permission to shoot rabbits, so the police probably wouldn't be interested."

"But it's horrible," said Emma. "And I'm going to write about it in my school project."

"That's probably the best thing you can do," said Mom. "After all, it's part of living in the country."

The next morning, Emma and Sheltie went to the woods again. Emma was hoping to see the same man out shooting so that she could take his photograph for her school project. But he was nowhere to be seen.

Sheltie kept a sharp lookout, too, but the woods were empty. Yet as they wandered around, Emma had a strange feeling that she was being watched. Sheltie seemed to sense it, too, and kept looking back over his shoulder and blowing funny little snorts.

Every now and then, Emma heard movement in the undergrowth. It was as if something was following them but didn't want to be seen.

The rustling seemed to be getting nearer and nearer. Sheltie was taking long sniffs and becoming quite restless.

"It must be some kind of animal," whispered Emma, "but why is it following us? And why is it hiding?"

Sheltie listened to Emma's voice and

whinnied softly. He didn't understand what Emma was saying but he *did* know that something was hiding out there.

Emma slid quietly from the saddle and crouched low on the ground. She peered under the bushes from a distance, to try to see if she could spot anything.

Emma wasn't scared. She knew that foxes and badgers didn't attack people. They were more likely to run away if they saw a human. And rabbits and squirrels could sometimes be curious, but Emma had never heard of them following anyone before. As far as Emma knew, there were no dangerous animals living in the woods.

Even so, there was definitely something there and Emma was going to find out exactly what it was.

She smiled happily. "You stay right here,

Sheltie," she said. Then she began to crawl
toward the bushes.

Suddenly, something shot out of the
bush in front of her. Emma's scream echoed
through the woods.

Chapter Two

Emma gasped with surprise as a black-and-white dog jumped up on her. Sheltie blew a snort and Emma laughed as the little dog began licking her face with its soft pink tongue.

Sheltie pushed his nose forward and nuzzled the dog's head. Then the dog began covering Sheltie's face with kisses, too.

Emma tried to hold the dog, but it

wriggled like a worm in her arms.
Suddenly, the little dog seemed frightened
and ran away, back into the woods.

"Where on earth did *that* come from?"
said Emma. "Did you see where it went,
Sheltie?"

The little pony pawed at the ground with
his hoof and stared through the trees into
the woods.

"Do you think we might find it again, boy? Maybe it's lost. Or its owner's in trouble."

Sheltie's answer was to stomp the ground with his hooves.

"Come on, then, Sheltie. Let's go take a look." Emma climbed back into the saddle and walked Sheltie farther into the woods.

They searched and searched but they didn't find anything. Emma called out, in case someone needed help: "Hello! Hello!" But there was no answer.

She called to the dog. Sheltie called, too, by neighing loudly. But the little dog didn't return.

"Maybe it lives nearby and has just taken itself out for a walk," said Emma. "It's probably gone back home now!"

But Sheltie didn't seem to think so. As

they left the woods, he became fidgety and kept swinging his head around to look back into the trees.

"Another day with no photographs," said Emma. "Maybe we'll be luckier tomorrow!"

But the next day it was raining and Emma didn't go out riding at all.

At breakfast, Mom asked Emma, "Have you been out to feed Sheltie yet?"

"No," said Emma. "I thought I would wait a while until the rain stops."

Emma's little brother, Joshua, was playing with a model pony, galloping it up and down the arm of his highchair. When he heard Sheltie's name, he looked up and laughed. "Sheltie!" he said, and continued playing.

"So you haven't been out this morning, then, Emma?" said Mom. "It's just that the milk bottle was knocked over outside on the step and I wondered if you knew anything about it."

In between mouthfuls of cereal, Emma said, "No, I don't, Mom. I haven't been outside at all."

"And Sheltie hasn't escaped, has he?" Mom asked.

"No. He's standing in the paddock waiting for his breakfast," said Emma. "Why?"

"Well, the milk bottle wasn't just knocked over. All the milk had disappeared, too!"

"Couldn't it just have gotten washed away by the rain?" said Dad, looking up from his newspaper.

"Not really," answered Mom. "The back step's under the cover of the porch roof. And there would at least be a small puddle of milk or something! No. It looked as though it had been deliberately spilled and then drunk. There wasn't a trace of milk left, except for a few drops inside the bottle."

"Sometimes small birds peck the tops off milk bottles and drink the cream," said Dad.

"But I've never known one to tip a bottle over and drink the whole pint." Mom laughed.

"Maybe it was a great big bird," said Emma. "Like an ostrich!"

Mom burst out laughing. "I don't think there are many ostriches running loose in Little Applewood," she said. "And if there were, I'm sure we would have noticed!"

"Then it's a mystery!" announced Emma. She loved mysteries.

The next day was Saturday and Emma decided to get up extra early and wait for the milk to be delivered. Whoever was stealing the milk, Emma was determined to catch them in the act and take a photograph of them doing it.

That would be an unusual story to write about for her school wildlife project. Emma was certain of it!

Chapter Three

On Saturday morning, as planned, Emma woke to the sound of her alarm clock, which she had set for earlier than usual. *Beep! Beep! Beep!* She sat up in bed and switched it off.

Emma dressed quickly and pulled on an extra sweater. It felt really cold this morning. "OK!" she said. "I'm ready."

Emma grabbed her camera and tiptoed downstairs. It was already light as she unlocked the back door and slipped outside. She knew the milkman would be coming in about five minutes.

Sheltie looked surprised to see Emma up so early. He blew a loud snort and came trotting over to the paddock gate from his field shelter.

"Don't get too excited," called Emma. "We're not going anywhere." She leaned over the fence and rubbed his neck.

Sheltie pushed his muzzle into Emma's soft sweater and made snuffly pony noises. Then he watched as Emma ran back up the yard to the tack room. Sheltie wondered what she was up to!

He watched Emma open the tack room door and slip inside. She left the door ajar and poked her head around the side. Emma was hiding.

Sheltie could still see her and whinnied excitedly. He thought this was some kind of new game. But Emma didn't come out. She stayed in her hiding place and waited.

A few minutes later, the milkman arrived. He rolled up in his little white van, then walked up the path to deliver two pints of milk. This morning, he brought a loaf of bread, too.

Emma and Sheltie watched as the milkman left the milk bottles and bread on the back doorstep. Then he strolled back down the path, whistling to himself.

"Good morning, Sheltie," he called out, and waved to the little Shetland pony. Sheltie answered by blowing a loud raspberry. Emma giggled from her hiding place. The milkman hadn't seen her.

Emma got ready with her camera.

"Come on, ostrich, or whatever you are. I'm waiting!" Emma could see the doorstep quite clearly from the tack room and was close enough to get a good shot with her camera.

Suddenly, Sheltie started acting up. He was blowing hard and snorting and stomping his feet on the grass. Sheltie had seen something.

He lowered his head and watched a small shape go slinking by alongside the garden hedge. Something hairy. Something black and white.

Emma saw it, too, as it slipped through a gap and padded up the path toward the back door.

It wasn't anything strange like an ostrich. Emma had known it wouldn't be, really. It was the little dog they had met in the woods!

Emma watched with her camera poised as it found the loaf of bread and began to tear hungrily at the plastic wrapper.

The poor thing must be starving, thought Emma. She kept still and watched the dog eat the slices of bread. It wolfed down half the loaf before it looked up, licking its lips. Then it pushed over a milk bottle, used its teeth to pull off the thin silver top, and lapped up the spilled milk.

Click! Whirr! Emma took a photograph. She had solved the mystery and caught the culprit on film.

The little dog was startled by the sudden noise and pricked up its floppy ears. Emma came out of hiding to try and make friends. But the little dog got scared and ran away, leaving the empty bottle and the half-eaten loaf behind.

Emma watched as the dog took off down the path, through the hedge, and away up the road.

Sheltie watched it, too, and whinnied as

if to say, "Come back, we won't hurt you!"
But the dog had gone.

Emma ran back inside the house to tell
Mom and Dad. She bounded up the stairs
and burst into her parents' bedroom. Then

she bounced onto their bed and woke them both up with a start.

"It's a dog!" she cried. "A little black-and-white dog. I saw it drink the milk and eat our bread."

Mom rubbed the sleep from her eyes.

"What *are* you talking about, Emma?" she said.

Dad moaned and pulled the covers up over his head.

"The milk thief!" exclaimed Emma. "It's a dog. And it was starving! It ate the bread and drank the milk and I've got a photo to prove it!"

Mom made Emma explain exactly what had happened. By now, Joshua was awake. He heard all the talking and tottered into the bedroom to see what was going on. Mom lifted him up onto the bed and he snuggled down between his parents.

With all the excitement, Mom was wide awake. She and Emma got up and left Dad and Joshua to doze.

Downstairs, while Mom made some coffee, Emma told how she had seen the little dog two days earlier in the woods.

"It must belong to someone," said Mom.

"But what if it doesn't?" said Emma. "What if it's lost or it's been thrown out of its home and is living wild? It's such a cute little dog. It must be so lonely living out in the woods all on its own!"

"Did it have a collar?" asked Mom.

"I don't know," answered Emma. "I didn't see one."

"Well, maybe after breakfast you can take Sheltie out into the woods to look for it. If it's a stray, we should try to catch it. We can't have a dog living wild in Little Applewood. It might start bothering Mr. Brown's sheep."

"Oh! I'm sure it wouldn't harm any sheep," said Emma. "It's such a nice, friendly dog. It must have followed me and Sheltie the other morning and seen where we live. It's just hungry and probably scared and lonely, too!"

"Well, if you *do* see it again, don't touch it, in case it bites," said Mom, worried.

"But it doesn't," interrupted Emma. "It licks and licks and licks. It's really friendly. Honest!"

"Emma!" Mom said sternly. She gave Emma a "do as you're told" look.

"All right. If I find it, I'll come back and tell you. Or I could get it to follow me home!" she added brightly.

"I'll give you a box of crackers, to take with you in case you do see it again," said Mom. "Maybe it would be best if you *could* get it to follow you home. Then we can decide what to do with it."

"We could keep it!" said Emma. "It's such a sweet little dog."

"I don't know about that, Emma," said Mom. "But we could try to find it a nice home. Now help me upstairs with this coffee."

Mom climbed back into bed with Dad and Joshua. But Emma was wide awake. She couldn't wait for breakfast time so she helped herself to cereal in the kitchen. Then she took the crackers Mom had left out for her and stuffed them into her coat pocket.

"I'm taking Sheltie over to Sally's," Emma called up the stairs. "Then we'll ride through the woods to look for Scamp." Scamp was the name Emma had already given the stray dog. Emma thought it looked like a mischievous little scamp.

"OK," answered Mom. "But be back for lunch. And remember, Emma, if you *do* find the dog, don't touch it!"

Chapter Four

Sally was Emma's best friend. She had a pony of her own. He was named Minnow. Sheltie and Minnow were friends, too. Sally lived in Fox Hall Manor, just a short ride away.

It was still early when Emma and Sheltie trotted through the big iron gates of the manor. But Sally was already up and tending to Minnow in his stable at the back of the house.

"Hi, Sally," called Emma. Sheltie blew a good-morning snort, and Minnow answered with a soft whinny.

"You're an early bird!" said Sally. "It's only eight o'clock."

"We're on pony patrol this morning," said Emma cheerfully. "There's a stray dog living in Bramble Wood and we've got to find it!"

"A stray dog!" echoed Sally.

Emma told Sally all about Scamp while she tacked up Minnow.

"It's no more than a puppy, really," said Emma, "and it's so cute and cuddly. If we find it, I'm going to tempt it back to the house with some crackers." Emma patted her jacket pocket.

When Sheltie heard the cracker packet rustling, his ears pricked up.

"They're not for you, greedy." Emma laughed.

Sheltie lowered his head and whinnied sulkily.

"Well, maybe one, then," added Emma. "But not yet. You have to help us find Scamp first!"

Sheltie pricked up his ears again and began prancing on the spot.

"Come on, then," said Sally. "Let's get going!"

They set off at a steady walk until they reached Mr. Brown's meadow. Then they stretched their ponies and cantered across the open field to the edge of the woods.

"Where did you first see Scamp?" asked Sally.

"In the woods up on the old bridle path," said Emma. "The one that leads out to the meadow. I thought it would be a good idea if we went there first."

Sheltie and Minnow walked the path side by side, blowing puffs of steam and rustling their hooves through drifts of fallen leaves.

"The woods always look different when the leaves come down," said Sally. "You can see much farther through the trees.

35

Look, you can even see that man all the way over there!"

Emma looked across to where Sally was pointing. In the distance, some way off, walking through the trees, was a man with a shotgun cocked across his arm.

Emma recognized him right away. It was the same man she had seen three days earlier.

Emma didn't like riding anywhere near him, so she said to Sally, "Why don't we go up to the back woods? We never ride up there."

"It's worth a look," said Sally. "There's no sign of a dog anywhere around here, is there?"

"Maybe Sheltie can help us find it," said Emma. She leaned forward across Sheltie's neck and whispered in his ear, "Can you help us find Scamp, Sheltie?" Then she rustled the crackers.

Sheltie couldn't understand *exactly* what Emma was saying, but he seemed to know that they were looking for something. And maybe there was a treat for him at the end of it!

Sheltie raised his nose in the air and took a long, deep sniff. Then he blew a sharp snort that made Minnow jump.

They searched the back woods but found nothing until Sheltie led them down into a gully and suddenly stopped by an old drainpipe. The concrete pipe was almost one yard across and stuck out of a steep bank.

Sheltie pawed at the ground with his hoof, then lowered his head slightly to peer inside the drainpipe.

"Sheltie's found something!" exclaimed Emma.

Sheltie blew a snort of triumph, which was answered with a soft bark.

"Did you hear that?" said Emma. Sally nodded. Emma slid from her saddle.

Sheltie was trying to push his head inside the drainpipe for a better look.

"Come away, Sheltie." Emma coaxed her little pony away from the drainpipe, then crouched down herself to peer inside.

No sooner had Emma knelt in front of the opening than the little dog jumped out at her. It covered her face with kisses. And no matter how hard Emma tried not to break her promise to Mom, she couldn't help it. Emma threw her arms around

Scamp and gave the little dog the biggest
cuddle it had ever had.

Sally dismounted, too, and petted the
cute stray.

Emma opened the packet of crackers and
watched in amazement as Scamp started to
wolf down all of them.

"Save some for Sheltie," said Sally.

Emma grinned. "I already did." She thrust her hand into her pocket and produced four crackers.

"Two for Sheltie," she said, "and two for Minnow."

Scamp looked up and watched Sheltie and Minnow gobble down their treats. Then he looked up at Emma with big, cute eyes as if to say, "Are there any more?"

"Come on, Scamp," said Emma. "The plan is that you're supposed to follow us back to the house."

Scamp wagged his tail. Then he stood up on his hind legs and licked the crumbs from Sheltie's nose.

"I think Scamp will follow you two anywhere," said Sally.

Chapter Five

From the front gate, Mom watched Emma and Sheltie lead the little stray dog up the road. Sally and Minnow rode a little way behind them.

Scamp looked nervous, but he seemed happy to follow at Sheltie's heels as they trotted along.

Joshua stood with Mom and pointed through the gate.

"Woof, woof," he said.

"Yes, woof, woof," said Mom. "It's a little dog, but we don't want to scare him, Joshua. We've got to be very quiet."

Joshua put his finger to his lips and said, "Shh!"

Then they watched as Scamp followed Sheltie up the path to the paddock.

Mom came through the gate to greet Scamp. And Joshua stood behind her, peering between her legs.

The little dog looked at them both. Then he looked back at Sally and Minnow. Finally, he looked at Emma and Sheltie, then gave a little whine before he ran off as fast as his legs would carry him.

Everyone watched in amazement as the little dog shot back up the road like a rocket.

Emma was so disappointed.

"Oh, no!" she wailed. "He followed us all the way from the woods and now he's run off!"

"He probably got frightened," said Mom. "Seeing everybody at once must have spooked him."

"Should we go see if we can find him again?" said Sally.

Mom thought about it for a moment, then said, "It's probably best to just leave it for now. The dog knows where we are. We'll leave some food and water out and see what happens."

Sally glanced at her watch.

"I'd better be going," she announced. "Mom's taking me into town after lunch to buy new shoes."

Emma made a face.

"I know!" said Sally. "But I've got to go."

"I'll call you tomorrow," said Emma, and waved as Sally took Minnow off at a fast walk.

After Sally had gone, Emma turned to Mom.

"Do you think Scamp will come back?" she asked.

"He might," said Mom. "We'll go into

the village after lunch and buy some dog food. Something nice and tasty to tempt a hungry stray."

That night, before they went to bed, Mom left a bowl of dog food and a bowl of water on the back step.

"I hope Scamp finds his way back," said Emma.

Mom brushed the hair out of Emma's eyes and pulled the blankets up, tucking her in nice and warm.

"Let's see what tomorrow brings," said Mom.

The next morning, Emma woke to the sound of the church bells ringing from the village.

She sat up in bed and counted the chimes.

"Eight!" There were eight chimes. Emma
threw back the blankets and grabbed her
warm robe. She made her bed, washed,
and then dressed before she hurried
downstairs.

When Emma unlocked the back door
and peered out onto the step, a contented
smile swept across her face.

The two bowls were empty. Scamp must have come for the food and water.

Emma looked around, but there was no sign of the little dog. She glanced down to the paddock. There was no sign of Sheltie, either.

Suddenly, Emma was concerned. Sheltie was *always* waiting for her at the paddock gate. But this morning he wasn't there. Where *was* he?

Chapter Six

Emma climbed the paddock fence and hurried across to Sheltie's field shelter. As she peered inside, Emma let out a sigh of relief. Sheltie was lying down on the straw. And there, snuggled between his forelegs, was Scamp, the little stray dog, curled up fast asleep.

Sheltie whinnied softly. It was as though the little pony didn't want to wake his new

friend. Emma looked down at her Shetland
pony and the little lost stray.

"Don't worry, Scamp," whispered
Emma. "We'll take care of you."

The little dog opened one lazy eye and
gazed up at Emma. Emma half expected

Scamp to run off again as he had before. But he didn't. He just closed his eyes and gave a contented grunt. Then he went back to sleep.

Emma ran all the way back to the house. Mom and Dad were both in the kitchen setting the table with cups and breakfast plates.

"Come quickly," said Emma. "It's Scamp! He's in the shelter curled up asleep with Sheltie. He came back all on his own!"

Dad acted quickly. "You stay here with Joshua," he said to Mom. "I'll use one of my old ties to make a leash. Come on, Emma." Soon they were off, hurrying down to the paddock.

Emma and Dad poked their heads slowly around the shelter wall and peered inside. Sheltie was still lying on the straw, with Scamp fast asleep between his forelegs.

When Sheltie saw Emma, he whinnied softly again.

"Shh, Sheltie!" said Dad. He didn't want the little dog to wake up. But it was too late. Suddenly, Scamp sat upright and gave a little woof.

Emma crouched down and stretched out her arm toward him. Scamp wagged his tail and licked the back of Emma's hand with his warm, smooth tongue.

"Here," whispered Dad. "Slip this tie over his head."

Scamp sat very still and made no fuss at all as Emma slipped the makeshift leash around his neck.

Sheltie blew a snort of triumph and jiggled to his feet. Then he shook out his mane and showered Scamp with straw.

Emma stroked the little dog and Dad made friends with him, too. Then they led Scamp up to the house to a nice warm kitchen and a handful of dog biscuits.

"He *must* belong to someone," said Mom as she handed Joshua a piece of toast spread with honey.

"Nice doggy," said Joshua. And he threw the toast on the floor in front of Scamp. Emma giggled as the little dog wolfed it down.

"No, Joshua," said Mom. "You shouldn't do that!" Then she buttered another piece of toast for Emma's little brother before turning her attention back to Scamp.

"He must belong to someone," she said again. "We'll have to ask around. Will you take Sheltie and ride up to Marjorie Wallace's, Emma? She might know if anyone's lost a dog."

"That's a good idea," agreed Emma. "I'll get Sally and Minnow to come, too! We can stop at all the houses on the way. If Scamp's missing from his home, then *someone* may know him!"

Later that morning, Emma and Sally rode all over Little Applewood. The day was bright and sunny, but there was a chilly breeze in the air.

Sheltie and Minnow trotted along happily side by side. Every now and then, they came across a deep drift of autumn

53

leaves. Then Sheltie would rustle through them, lifting his hooves high and trampling as many leaves as he could.

"Sheltie's so funny." Sally laughed. "He's always full of mischief, isn't he?"

"That's just how I like him," said Emma, grinning.

They rode on, up to Marjorie Wallace's place. Marjorie had nine cats and took care of all kinds of rescued animals. She hadn't heard of anyone who had *lost* a dog, but she knew of someone who was missing one.

"It's such a shame," began Marjorie. "Poor old Fred Berry. He had a dog named Jasper who died last week of old age. Poor Fred is heartbroken, he misses that dog so much."

Emma felt really sad for Fred. She tried

to imagine what it would feel like if
anything happened to Sheltie!

"If I hear of anyone who has lost a dog,
though, I'll let you know," said Marjorie.

Emma and Sally rode away. And at
every house they visited, it was the same.

No one had heard of anyone who had lost a dog.

Back at home, Mom decided that it would be a good idea to put a sign in the post-office window first thing Monday morning.

Emma knew that it was the right thing to do. But secretly she still wished that she could keep Scamp for herself.

By lunchtime the next day, Mom's sign was in the post-office window. Emma saw it on her way home from school. It read:

FOUND

Young, black-and-white, long-haired dog.

Very friendly. Rescued from Bramble Wood.

Contact . . .

Then it gave their address and telephone number.

"Has anyone called about Scamp?" asked Emma.

"It's early still," said Mom. "The sign only went up this afternoon."

The little dog was curled up warm and cozy in a cardboard box next to the kitchen stove. When he heard Emma come in, he bounded across the floor.

"Come on, Scamp," Emma said. "I'll take you for a nice walk before it gets dark."

Mom had borrowed a real collar and leash from a friend in the village. Scamp's tail thumped the floor as Emma slipped it on.

Emma tied Scamp outside while she fitted Sheltie's halter and lead rein. Then she took both of them for a stroll before dinner.

On the way, they bumped into Fred Berry. Fred used to walk Jasper every day at that time. He looked sad and lonely without his little friend.

"Hello, Emma. Hello, Sheltie," he said. "And who's this? What a great dog! Where on earth did you find him?"

Emma told Fred Berry all about Scamp.

"Well, I hope you find his owner soon," he said. "It's an awful thing when you lose an animal."

Emma knew that Fred was missing Jasper. But she still didn't really want to find Scamp's owner. Emma kept hoping that she would be able to keep him.

Sheltie liked Scamp, too! The whole time as they walked along, Sheltie kept nuzzling the little dog's head and making friendly whinnies.

"If no one comes forward," Emma said to Scamp, "then we'll *have* to keep you."

But when Emma got back to the house, she found that Mom had other plans.

Chapter Seven

"If we don't hear from anyone by the end of the week," said Mom, "maybe we should put an ad in the local paper."

Oh, no, thought Emma. That meant more people would know about Scamp. And more people meant less chance of Scamp staying.

By Thursday, when Emma got home from school, there were still no calls about Scamp. Scamp had settled in nicely and

Emma knew that it was going to be really hard to give him up.

"I put a 'found' notice in the *County Gazette* today," said Mom. "It should be in the paper tomorrow, so we might hear something from Scamp's owner over the weekend."

Emma didn't want to hear anything from Scamp's owner at *any* time. For almost a whole week she had been able to pretend that Scamp belonged to her.

Of course, Emma knew it was right to try to find Scamp's owner. But she had grown so fond of the little dog, and so had Sheltie.

Over the last two days, Emma had taught Scamp to walk alongside Sheltie on a long leash. And Sheltie had seemed to love having the little dog padding along next to him as they walked the roads.

Scamp jumped up at Emma and cocked his head to one side. Emma scratched his ears and said, "Don't worry, boy. Maybe no one will answer the ad. Then you can live here forever!"

Mom pretended she didn't hear Emma but gave Dad a funny look and raised one eyebrow.

"I'll take Scamp out for a walk with Sheltie before dinner," Emma announced. She dashed upstairs to change out of her school clothes, then clipped the long leash onto Scamp's collar and rushed through the yard.

When Sheltie saw Emma and Scamp coming, he did a mad dash around the paddock, kicking his heels and snorting loudly.

Emma tied Scamp to the fence while she tacked up Sheltie. The little dog was happy to scamper and roll among the leaves while he waited.

Then Emma unlocked the gate and mounted Sheltie. She took hold of Scamp's long leash and they had a nice long walk up the road and across Mr. Brown's meadow to Horseshoe Pond and back.

Later, when they were all settled at the kitchen table having their dinner, Mom had a talk with Emma.

"I know it's going to be hard," said Mom, "but if Scamp's owner *does* turn up, we'll have to let him go."

Emma looked down at her plate and poked at her sausages with her fork.

"But what if nobody turns up to claim Scamp?" she asked. "Can we keep him?"

Mom looked across at Dad. Then Dad spoke.

"Well, Emma," he began. "Keeping a dog is a huge responsibility. I'm working all week and Mom is busy looking after Joshua and helping out at the craft shop. And you're at school all day. I don't know if we *can* look after a dog as well!"

Suddenly, Emma felt very sad. "But he needs a good home," she said.

"Oh, we'll make certain he finds a good home," said Mom, "but it might not be here with us."

Scamp cocked his head to one side as if he were listening to every word.

"Sheltie could look after him when there's no one here," Emma suggested.

"I don't think so, Emma," said Dad kindly. "It wouldn't be fair to Scamp. He needs someone to look after him all day long. Like ponies, dogs can be a handful."

Emma finished her dinner in silence.

On Saturday morning, Emma took Sheltie and Scamp out for a walk again.

But this time, when they came home, there was a car parked outside the house. One of the car doors was open and a man was standing there talking to Dad.

Emma recognized the man at once and felt a twinge of panic. It was the same man she had seen in the woods, carrying a shotgun.

Scamp recognized the man, too, and began to whine and pull on his leash in alarm.

Emma quickly turned Sheltie out into the paddock and held on tightly to Scamp. The little dog was fretting and squirming to free himself from his collar.

Emma stood a little way off and listened to what the man was saying. He looked across at Emma and Scamp.

"There he is. There's my dog!" the man said in a very loud voice. "I saw the ad in the papers this morning and came over as soon as I could."

Emma's heart skipped a beat. *This man couldn't possibly be Scamp's owner,* she thought. But somehow she knew that it was true.

"I live in Rilport, but I was over here last week with the dog and he ran off. I've been looking everywhere for him ever since."

It sounded horribly true. Emma didn't want to believe it, but the man had come to take Scamp away.

Dad stood talking with the man, checking over his story and asking questions. And the whole time Scamp tried to hide behind Emma's legs. The poor dog was trembling from head to tail.

Then the man produced a piece of paper showing that he had paid twenty dollars for Scamp at a farm.

"That's my dog," said the man flatly. "Now hand him over."

It was hopeless; there was nothing they could do.

"How do you know he's your dog?" asked Emma. "You haven't even looked at him closely. There are probably hundreds

of black-and-white dogs around just like
this one!"

"But I just told you, I lost him in the
woods up there. And that's where you

found him. Anyway, I'd recognize him anywhere." The man was beginning to sound really angry.

Dad didn't like his tone of voice. And judging by the way the dog was behaving, neither did Scamp. But there was nothing Dad could do.

"I'm afraid we'll have to give Scamp back, Emma," said Dad gently. "Why don't you carry him over to the car and say good-bye?"

Emma didn't want to, but she scooped Scamp up in her arms and carried him across to the waiting car.

Then Emma did something very risky. As she put Scamp down on the car seat, she deliberately unclipped the dog's leash.

Scamp seemed to know exactly what

was happening. As soon as the leash came free, he jumped from the car and bounded away, running as fast as his legs would carry him. Emma watched Scamp dash through a gap in the hedge and scoot across Sheltie's paddock.

When he got to the other side, he squeezed through the fenceposts and disappeared.

"You thoughtless girl!" yelled the man. "You did that on purpose!"

But Emma didn't care. Dad half grinned and said it was obviously an accident. The man's face turned bright red and he stormed off back to his car. Emma ran indoors. She thought she was in big trouble.

Emma peered through the kitchen window and saw Dad outside talking to the man. Then the man drove away and Dad walked back to the house.

I'm in trouble now! thought Emma.

Chapter Eight

"What a nasty man!" said Dad as he stepped into the kitchen. Emma was expecting to be scolded, but Dad just smiled. "Don't worry, Emma," he said. "I don't think that man really wanted Scamp back, anyway. He'd rather have a mean, rough dog. What you did was wrong. But I don't blame you. I gave the man the twenty dollars he paid for Scamp, and he's gone for good, I promise you!"

Emma's face lit up.

"Oh, Dad! Does that mean we can keep him?" she asked.

"Well, not exactly," said Dad. "But at least Scamp won't be going to live with someone who doesn't really want him. Now, why don't you take Sheltie and go see if you can find Scamp? Let's just hope he hasn't gone too far."

Emma didn't need to be told twice. She ran to the paddock, mounted Sheltie, and took off at a fast trot to find the little dog.

Emma searched everywhere for Scamp. She rode through the woods calling his name, but she couldn't see him anywhere.

"Where could he have gone?" said Emma.

Sheltie blew a snort and pawed at the ground. He tossed his head and looked around. Sheltie was searching for Scamp, too!

"I bet *you* know where he's hiding, don't you, boy?" said Emma.

Sheltie lifted his head and sniffed the cold, frosty air.

"Go on, then," Emma urged. "Find Scamp!"

Emma squeezed Sheltie's sides with her legs and loosened his reins. This was Emma's signal for Sheltie to go where he wanted.

The little Shetland took off immediately. He snorted and sniffed at the air as he hurriedly walked the bridle path.

Then, suddenly, Sheltie changed direction and turned to head for the back woods.

Sheltie quickened his pace and bounced along, trampling through the leaves.

Once in the back woods, Sheltie made his way to the gully where they had first found Scamp. He stopped at the drainpipe and Emma jumped down from the saddle.

"Great job, Sheltie," she said, and patted his neck.

Then, as Emma crouched to peer inside, Sheltie blew a snort and Emma heard a sad whine coming from far back inside the concrete pipe.

"Scamp!" called Emma, in no more than a hushed whisper. "Come out, boy. You're safe now. Here, Scamp! Here, boy!"

The little dog was definitely inside. Emma could hear him whimpering quite clearly. But Scamp was terrified and wouldn't come out.

"Looks like I'll just have to go in and get him, Sheltie," said Emma, and she began to crawl inside.

As soon as Emma entered the pipe, she felt it move slightly under her weight. Emma stopped for a moment. Cautiously, she rocked gently from side to side on her hands and knees. The pipe seemed solid enough.

Emma crept forward, whispering, "Here, boy. It's me, Emma. Don't be scared. I'm coming to get you!"

As she crawled forward, the pipe moved again. Only a little bit, but it seemed to dip in front of her.

Emma could see Scamp now, hiding in the gloom only a few feet ahead of her. She could also see why Scamp hadn't gone any farther. Behind him, the pipe had collapsed and was blocked and choked with tree roots. *It must have been like that for ages*, thought Emma.

She crawled forward and reached out with her hand. She could almost touch Scamp now.

Just a little farther and Emma felt his warm, soft tongue licking her hand. Then he came forward and Emma gave him a hug.

She took hold of Scamp's collar and turned around in the pipe, ready to clip on his long leash to help the little dog out. Emma could see Sheltie at the end of the dark tunnel, peering in.

"We're coming, Sheltie," she called. "I've got him!"

But just then, the pipe moved, and before Emma could crawl out, the entrance collapsed. A big piece of concrete came down with a crash and blocked her exit.

Emma screamed. Sheltie jumped back and blew a loud snort. The entrance to the drain was no more than a small hole now, but Sheltie knew that Emma was inside.

He pawed at the ground frantically as
Emma's face appeared at the small
opening. The hole was large enough to
look through but far too small to crawl out
of. Emma didn't want to try and move
anything in case it made things worse.

Instead, she looked to Sheltie for help.

"Go get Dad, Sheltie," she called. "Get
Dad! Quickly!"

Sheltie stood looking at Emma's face
peering out of the small hole in the pipe.
He cocked his head to one side, listening.

"Go on," urged Emma again. "Get help,
Sheltie. Go get Dad!"

Sheltie flicked his tail, then turned and
galloped back through the woods as fast as
he could, kicking up piles of leaves.

Emma sat very still. She hugged Scamp on her lap and waited. She was too scared to move in case the drain shifted again and collapsed on top of her. Emma hoped it wouldn't be long before Sheltie brought help.

Chapter Nine

Sheltie galloped all the way through the woods without stopping, until he found someone who could help. But it wasn't Dad. It was Fred Berry, out on one of his walks.

"Hello, Sheltie," said Fred. "What are you doing out here all on your own? Where's Emma?" He spoke gently as he took up the pony's reins.

Sheltie whinnied loudly and blew puffs

of steam into the cold air. Fred knew right away that something was wrong. Sheltie was already pulling Fred along, urging him to hurry.

"Go on, then, Sheltie. Take me to Emma."

Fred let go of the reins and Sheltie took off down the road. Fred followed at a run and did his best to keep up. Before long, he was huffing and puffing his way through the back woods and stumbling after Sheltie into the gully. The whole time, he was calling out Emma's name.

"Emma! Emma!" His voice echoed through the trees. Emma heard him and yelled back.

"Over here, I'm in here! I'm trapped in a big pipe."

Scamp heard Fred, too, and started

barking. Sheltie showed Fred the collapsed drain and when Fred saw it, he gasped.

"Emma, are you all right?" he said.

"Yes, we're OK," answered Emma.

"Whatever you do, don't make any sudden movements," said Fred. He peered through the opening. "Slide back slowly into the pipe and keep a tight hold on Scamp."

Emma did as she was told and Fred started to pull at the concrete blocking the entrance.

The piece of drain that had collapsed was very heavy. It moved slightly but Fred wasn't quite strong enough to pull it free. He needed some help. But he didn't want to leave Emma alone and trapped inside.

Then Sheltie blew a really loud snort and nudged Fred gently in the small of his back. He seemed to be telling Fred that he could help.

Fred looked at Sheltie. Then he had an idea.

"If only I had a rope or something, Emma, then I could tie it to the broken pipe and get Sheltie to help me pull it free! But where will I find a rope?"

"There's a rope tied to Sheltie's saddle," yelled Emma. "And I've got a long leash in here, too!" She crawled forward carefully and passed the long leather leash through the hole.

Fred tied the leash around the piece of pipe and looped the rope through it. He then fixed the rope to Sheltie's girth. Now there were two of them to pull.

"Ready, Sheltie?" said Fred.

Sheltie snorted and looked as though he was ready to pull. The little pony seemed to know exactly what he was expected to do.

Together, Fred and Sheltie pulled as hard as they could. The rope strained taut and suddenly, the broken pipe fell away as the rope pulled it free. Scamp bounded out and Emma escaped unhurt.

Sheltie did a little stomping dance and pushed his soft muzzle into Emma's tummy. Then he lowered his head and licked Scamp's ears. Scamp rolled over onto his back and wriggled his legs in the air.

Fred told Emma that she should never have crawled into the drainpipe.

"You should have gone for help," he said.

"But I couldn't leave Scamp," pleaded Emma. "He was so scared."

Scamp jumped up at Fred and licked his hand. Fred smiled and said, "Just what is Emma going to do with you, Scamp?"

Emma grinned. She understood now that they couldn't really keep Scamp at their house. The little dog could be quite a handful. He needed someone who could look after him all the time and train him properly. Someone who needed company as much as Scamp needed a home.

Then Emma had a wonderful idea!

Fred Berry was all alone in his house when Dad and Emma stopped by that afternoon. They also had Sheltie and Scamp with them. Fred seemed very pleased to have visitors.

Emma told Fred all about what had happened when they had found Scamp's owner.

". . . and we thought that if you liked the idea, then you could have Scamp to keep for your very own!" she said.

The old man was overjoyed. Scamp had already taken an instant liking to Fred and was curled up at his feet in front of the fire.

"I think I like that idea very much, Emma," said Fred. He had tears in his eyes as he spoke. "No one could ever replace Jasper, but I'm sure Scamp and I will be very happy together. He's a great little fella." Fred leaned forward and scratched Scamp's ears.

The little dog gave a sigh of contentment and fell fast asleep.

Emma took a photograph of Scamp and Fred.

"This will make a perfect ending for my 'Wildlife and Woodlands' project," she said.

Just then, Sheltie nudged the front door open and came clip-clopping through the door. He stood there looking at everyone, then blew a loud raspberry.

"Oh, Sheltie!" Emma giggled. "You were supposed to wait *outside*."

Fred Berry started to laugh as Emma went to grab Sheltie's reins. "He's a mischievous fellow, too, isn't he?" said Fred.

And with that, Sheltie snatched an apple from Fred's fruit bowl and dashed outside before Emma could reach him.

"Sheltie!" yelled Emma as she hurried outside. "Bring that back at once!" But Sheltie was already down at the end of Fred's yard, waiting for a game of tag.